Check out th̶ STI̶
∇ STI̶
Science ...̶iuon Titles!

How far would you go to break into
the movies? Get the answer in
BEHIND THE SCREAMS

Here today . . . gone tomorrow!
Find out more in
WARP WORLD 3030

It's alive. It's growing. It's *hungry*. See why in
BZZZZ

Earth is in for a big jolt. Check out why in
SHORT CIRCUIT

There's a whole lot of shakin' going on!
Read all about it in
SUPER STAR

What *are* those robots talking about?
Find out in
THE LOST LANGUAGE

All that glitters isn't good! See why in
CHARMERS

You may get more than you bargained for!
Check out
COSMIC EXCHANGE

This fan is out of this world!
Find out why in
ALIEN OBSESSION

ISBN 0-8114-9327-X
Copyright ©1995 Steck-Vaughn Company. All rights reserved. No part of the
material protected by this copyright may be reproduced or utilized in any form
or by any means, electronic or mechanical, including photocopying, recording,
or by any information storage and retrieval system, without permission in
writing from the copyright owner. Requests for permission to make copies of
any part of the work should be mailed to: Copyright Permissions, Steck-Vaughn
Company, P.O. Box 26015, Austin, TX 78755. Printed in the United States of
America.

  3 4 5 6 7 8 9 98

Produced by Mega-Books of New York, Inc.
Design and Art Direction by Michaelis/Carpelis Design Assoc.

Cover illustration: Ken Spencer

BLAST FROM THE PAST

by Pam Cardiff

interior illustrations by
Frank Mayo

STECK-VAUGHN
C O M P A N Y

Chapter · 1

"Hey, Manny!"

Manuel Trujillo looked up from his portable computer as his friend Richie Adair strolled up to him. Manny voice-commanded his computer to shut off, then called out a greeting. "Hey, Richie! What's up?"

It was noon and the Rockville High cafeteria was buzzing with noise and activity. Server robots were dishing up the hot meal of the day, chopped meat casserole, so there was a strong smell in the air, too.

"Here," said Manny, sliding his untouched plate toward Richie. "Try some chopped *feet* casserole."

Richie pushed the plate away and took a step backward. "Very funny, man," he said.

"Take a whiff," said Manny. "What do you think it is?"

Richie often wished he could rattle off wisecracks as easily as Manny did. Since Richie couldn't think of anything clever to say, he changed the subject. "Have you seen Cheryl?" he asked.

"It was her turn to go to the committee meeting, remember?" answered Manny. "She'll be here soon."

Manny, Richie, and their friend Cheryl Pinter were the sophomore members of the Rockville High Party Committee. There were also three juniors and three seniors on the committee. Twice a month the Party Committee threw a big bash for the whole school. The tickets they sold raised money for the Rockville High athletic program, which badly needed funds for equipment and events. So far, the parties that were organized by the juniors and seniors had all been great. But every sophomore party had been a bust.

"What do you think the theme of our next party will be?" asked Richie.

Manny shrugged his beefy shoulders. "Whatever it is, it can't be as bad as the Hawaiian luau," he said.

"Oh man, don't remind me," groaned Richie. "I don't want to see sand again until the summer . . . and not unless it's on a real beach."

"Whose idea was it to have sand all over the place, anyway?" asked Manny.

"Yours!" Richie replied. "You said we needed it for atmosphere."

"Well, it sure wasn't my idea to carry the sand in the same box as the food," said Manny.

Richie looked sheepishly at Manny. "I didn't know the bag would break and get sand all over the food!" he said.

Manny's round face crinkled into a

grin. "It was almost worth it to see the look on snobby Tonya Ling's face when she bit into her luau sandwich!" he chuckled.

"Hey, guys! What's so funny?" Cheryl plopped her books down on the lunchroom table. She ignored the fact that her tortoiseshell glasses had slid to the end of her nose.

"We were just discussing the

Hawaiian luau sand disaster," explained Manny.

"Ugh!" cried Cheryl. "I was picking sand out of my teeth for days!"

"You know," said Richie, "the luau really wasn't that bad if you compare it to our first party."

"The Barnyard Bash!" all three friends cried out together.

"Remember the band?" asked Cheryl.

"Farmer Izzy and the Squealing Piglets?" asked Manny. "I wish I could forget them. The refreshments were pretty good, though."

"Are you kidding?" exclaimed Richie. "Serving food from a pig trough was a disgusting idea, Manny. We should have talked you out of it."

"I thought it gave the party atmosphere," Manny argued.

"Let's talk about the atmosphere for our next party," said Cheryl, getting down to business. "Wait till you hear the theme."

Manny pounded a drumroll on the table. Cheryl picked up her electronic notebook, pushed her glasses back into position, and began to read.

"The next sophomore party will be on Saturday the 17th. It will have a rodeo theme."

"Rodeo?" asked Richie. "You mean one of those cowboy shows they used to have a long time ago? Didn't they outlaw those things because they were cruel to animals?"

"Some people thought they were," said Cheryl. "I don't know why they really stopped doing them. But anyway, the rodeo is our theme."

"Why did the committee pick something so outdated?" asked Manny.

"The old-fashioned parties have raised the most money," explained Cheryl. "That 'house party' the seniors threw last time had the biggest turnout yet. So anyway, let's meet after school to talk about our party."

The three friends agreed to meet after last period and walk over to Cheryl's house.

***

At 4 o'clock, Manny, Cheryl, and Richie were sprawled out on two long couches in Cheryl's basement. They were trying to figure out what to do about the rodeo party.

"What if we just give everybody cowboy hats to wear and decorate the gym to look like a corral?" asked Cheryl.

"Borrr-ring!" replied Manny. Then he noticed Richie poking through some boxes on the other side of the basement. "Richie!" he called. "This is your problem, too."

Richie ignored him, but a minute

later he called his friends. "Come here, you guys. Check this out!" Manny and Cheryl walked over.

Richie's tall, wiry body was bent over an old cardboard box. "Look at this stuff!" he said.

"Oh," said Cheryl indifferently. "Those are some of my dad's antiques. He's got a ton of junk down here."

"Do you know what all this stuff is?" asked Manny.

"It's nothing very interesting," she replied. "That thing's an old CD player. Look how big CDs used to be. These must be over four inches across! And this is a typewriter," Cheryl added. "I guess people used these in the days before computers."

"Wow!" said Richie. "This stuff must be a hundred years old!"

"Almost," answered Cheryl, bending down next to Richie. "The box is marked '1990s.' You know, there's much cooler stuff to look at down here. Did I ever show you guys my Great Uncle Zack's lab equipment?"

"No," replied Manny. "What was he, a scientist?"

"Yes, and a historian, too," Cheryl answered. She led the boys to the farthest corner of the basement. "My dad says Uncle Zack was a brilliant man. I never met him, though. He died before I was born."

"But your dad saved all his stuff?" asked Richie.

"Actually, it came with the house," said Cheryl. "Uncle Zack used to live here."

Cheryl moved aside a wooden folding screen, and there stood the remains of an old laboratory. Shelves and boxes were filled with all types of electronic equipment. There was also a large collection of old history books arranged in chronological order—from Ancient Greece to Great Twentieth Century Thinkers.

"Look, Manny," said Cheryl. "Here's a whole box of old computer stuff." Manny loved anything having to do with computers.

Richie reached into the box and pulled something out. "Cool!" he exclaimed, as his friends leaned in for a closer look. Richie was holding an old-fashioned computer keyboard.

Chapter · 2

"Look at that old thing!" Manny cried. "I wonder if there's anything I can hook it up to?"

Richie handed the keyboard to Manny and looked through the computer box. He found only a mouse, two broken screens and a box of old disks. "There's nothing good," he told Manny.

Cheryl pushed the computer box back against the wall. "Come on, you guys," she said. "You can look through this stuff another time. We still have a party to plan." She walked back to the couches and the boys followed. Manny brought the keyboard over with him.

"Now," said Cheryl, picking her

electronic notebook up off the floor. "We have to decide on decorations, food, and entertainment. Think 'Wild West,' you guys."

Manny absentmindedly typed WILD WEST on the keyboard. "Listen!" he

cried. A low-pitched hum was coming from the keyboard.

"Manny!" said Cheryl, fed up. "Will you give it up! It's just an old piece of junk. Come on."

"But listen," said Manny. "It's making a noise!"

"So what?" said Cheryl. "It can't do anything. Look, if this party stinks, no one's going to buy tickets to any other party we organize. We'll be total losers. So, are you going to help us or not?"

"Yeah, yeah," mumbled Manny.

"OK," said Cheryl. "What about this? Why don't one of you dress up like Jesse James? That might be cool."

"Who's he?" asked Manny. "A cowboy?"

"He wasn't a cowboy," Cheryl answered. "He was an outlaw. He and his men held up stagecoaches and trains and robbed banks back in the 1800s."

"Sounds like a great guy, Cheryl," said Richie sarcastically.

Manny was only half paying attention. He typed JESSE JAMES on the keyboard. Then, accidentally, his finger hit the ENTER key. The keyboard hummed loudly, then it made a sharp popping noise.

Out of nowhere, a man was suddenly standing in the room with the three teens. He was about 25 years old with longish hair and a beard. The man was wearing worn leather chaps over his pants, a leather vest and a dark, brimmed hat. A holster with two shiny handguns stuck out on either side.

"Jesse James!" cried Manny.

"What the . . .?" cried Jesse James.

"Manny, do something!" cried Cheryl.

"Now!" cried Richie.

Manny hit the DELETE key, but nothing happened. Jesse James looked confused. "Who are you varmints? Where am I?" he asked.

Manny tried to stay calm. "Okay," he thought to himself. "I entered JESSE

JAMES, hit the ENTER key, and Jesse appeared. Now I have to figure out how to make him disappear!" He typed in JESSE JAMES and hit the DELETE key. Immediately, the outlaw was gone.

"I've got it!" cried Manny. Just to be sure, he tried it again. He re-typed JESSE JAMES, hit ENTER—and there again stood the confused outlaw. A second later, Manny typed JESSE JAMES, hit DELETE, and Jesse was gone.

Cheryl took off her glasses and rubbed her pale green eyes. "Tell me what just happened," she said.

"Yeah," said Richie, looking curiously at Manny. "How did you do that?"

Manny explained about the ENTER and DELETE keys. "It's incredible!" he said. "I wonder if it works with objects, too, or just people?"

"Try it, man!" said Richie. "Type in a million dollars."

"Better make that three million,"

Cheryl chimed in.

Manny's fingers got busy. Nothing happened.

"Try typing in the Cosmic Cretins," said Richie, naming his favorite band. Manny typed.

"Nope," said Manny. "It didn't work."

"Wait," said Cheryl. "Uncle Zack was a history buff. Maybe it only works on people from the past. Try typing in The Beatles—you know, that group we were talking about in History of Music class."

23

Manny typed, and sure enough, the keyboard hummed and popped, and there stood four men with funny haircuts.

"The Beatles!" cried Cheryl.

"And you are . . . ?" asked the man twirling a pair of drumsticks with ring-filled fingers.

"It's a long story," said Manny. "We'll invite you back when we have time to explain. Later!" With that, Manny hit a few keys and The Beatles were gone.

"This is awesome!" said Cheryl. "Our problems are solved."

"What do you mean?" asked Richie.

"We can have the real Jesse James at our rodeo party," Cheryl replied. "It's going to be the coolest bash of 2075!"

Chapter · 3

Three weeks later, on the afternoon of the big rodeo bash, the gang met up at the virtual reality arcade. Cheryl was playing a game called *Mutants from Planet Gorgon*. She was sitting in a booth wearing special goggles that created the illusion of the mutants coming straight at her. Cheryl kept zapping the mutants on the screen with lasers. She was very intent on the game. Next to the booth, Richie and Manny were discussing the party.

"I don't know," Richie was saying. "Jesse looked pretty dangerous. Did you see those guns he was packing? Maybe we should bring back someone a little

friendlier for the party."

"Oh, come on," said Manny. "Nothing's going to happen. He only has to stick around for a little while—just long enough for everyone to get a good look at him."

Just then, Cheryl emerged from the *Mutants* booth. She took her glasses out of her pocket and put them on. Then she fluffed up her short blond hair, which had been plastered down by the

goggles. "The mutants got me," she said. "What are you guys up to?"

"I was just telling Manny I'm kind of worried about Jesse," Richie said. "He looked like one mean dude."

"Yeah," said Cheryl, "but did you see how confused he was? When we bring him back he won't know where he is or what's going on. That ought to keep him mellow."

"What if it makes him mad instead?" asked Richie.

"Then we just send him back!" Manny answered.

"Okay," said Richie, giving in. "I guess it will work. Now I'd better get going. I promised my mother I'd help her take some stuff to the recycling center."

"I've got to go, too," said Cheryl. "Let's meet at the gym at 6:30. That should give us enough time to set up."

"Don't forget the keyboard," said Manny.

Cheryl rolled her eyes at him. "Later."

At 6:35, Manny, Cheryl, and Richie were in the Rockville High gym. Richie and Manny were tacking up a mural their friend Raj had painted. It showed a cowboy riding a bucking bronco.

Cheryl was piling up cowboy hats and bandanas, which she would hand out to the party guests as they arrived. She had already set out platters of barbecued ribs, baked beans, salad and corn. When Cheryl finished with the hats, she walked over to where the guys were standing.

"I came up with a plan," she said. "After everyone arrives, I'll take the keyboard, go out into the hall and call up Jesse. Then I'll bring him in to the party. We'll let him hang out for a little while, then we'll lure him into the hall again and send him back."

"Sounds good," said Manny. Richie nodded in agreement.

A few minutes later, the guests began to arrive. Cheryl had gotten the old CD player from her uncle's stuff. She'd also found a CD of cowboy tunes. Richie went to set up the music.

Soon the gym was full. Kids were wearing the cowboy hats and bandanas and gnawing on ribs. Nothing had gone wrong, but no one looked like they were having much fun, either. Richie approached Manny, who was standing next to the food table.

"Cheryl went to her locker to get the keyboard," he whispered. "The guest of honor should be here in five minutes."

Meanwhile, Cheryl was pressing her right index finger to the sensor pad on the handle of her locker. The sensor registered her fingerprint and the locker sprang open. Cheryl grabbed her backpack which had the keyboard inside, and went to stand outside the gym. Manny poked his head out of the gym doors. "The coast is clear," he said. "Bring on the outlaw!"

Cheryl typed in JESSE JAMES and hit ENTER. The outlaw suddenly appeared. He was standing slightly crouched with his legs apart. He stared at Cheryl in shock and amazement. "Where's my horse?" he cried. "I was

riding my horse! What's going on here?"

"It's okay, Mr. James," said Cheryl in what she hoped was a soothing voice. "Just come with me."

To Cheryl's relief, Jesse followed her into the gym. As soon as they entered,

Manny stopped the music and picked up a microphone. "Listen up, everybody!" he said. "We have a special guest here tonight—the famous outlaw Jesse James!"

As the kids caught sight of Jesse a murmur went through the gym.

"Jesse James? Didn't he live, like, two hundred years ago?"

"Check out those boots!"

Everyone began to move in for a closer look. Manny caught Cheryl's eye and winked. Just then, someone screamed.

"Look!" Cheryl cried to Manny. She pointed in Jesse's direction.

Jesse stood backed up against the wall with a gun drawn. He swiveled his head from right to left, watching every movement in the room.

"All right, now," said Jesse, removing his hat. "Just hand over your money and your jewelry, real quiet-like, and nobody will get hurt."

"Get the keyboard. Things are out of control!" Richie whispered to Manny.

"We can't delete him right in front of everybody," Manny replied. "Besides, look! They think it's a joke!"

Sure enough, all the kids in the gym were laughing and chattering as they placed their wallets, watches, and jewelry into the hat Jesse was passing around.

"Quiet!" Jesse cried out suddenly. He looked mean. Cheryl was worried. Just how mean could an outlaw from the nineteenth century get? She had to think of something. Jesse's hat was overflowing with valuables. When a bunch of bangle bracelets clattered to the floor, Cheryl got an idea.

"Here, Mr. James, let me hold that for you," she said. "Manny, let Mr. James borrow your hat so he can fill that, too."

Jesse reluctantly handed Cheryl the hat full of loot.

Then he grabbed the cowboy hat Manny offered and continued making his rounds.

Soon the second hat was full.

"I'll keep this safe for you," said Manny, reaching for the second hat. Jesse allowed him to take it. "Don't try anything funny now, hear?" Jesse said. He kept his gun trained on Cheryl's and Manny's backs as he motioned them out the gym door.

While Jesse was collecting the valuables, Richie had dashed into the hallway and grabbed the keyboard. As soon as Jesse and the two others exited the gym, Richie punched in JESSE JAMES and hit the DELETE key. "Happy trails, Jesse," he said as the outlaw disappeared.

When Cheryl, Manny, and Richie re-
entered the gym with the hats full of
valuables, the other kids cheered.

"I think we did it," whispered Cheryl.
"We finally threw a decent party!"

Chapter · 4

That Monday, Cheryl met Richie and Manny in the school cafeteria. As usual, Manny had bought the hot lunch, then pushed it aside without eating it.

"Why don't you ever get the vegetarian special?" asked Cheryl, forking up some tofu-spinach lasagna. "It's a lot better than that mystery meat you waste your money on."

"I'm a carnivore, Cheryl," replied Manny. "If I ate nothing but veggies, I'd wilt. Hey, have you heard?" he continued. "We're the talk of the school. Jesse was a hit!"

"I know," said Cheryl. "I overheard some kids in my Electronics class this morning. They think Jesse was an actor. But they loved him!"

Richie nodded. "Kayla Jones asked me if Jesse was really anyone she knew," he said. "Some of the kids think he was Mr. Arnofsky, the Robotics teacher!"

Manny laughed along with the others. "Let them believe what they want," he said. "I don't think we should let anyone in on the real story."

"I'm with you, man," said Richie.

"Me, too," said Cheryl.

"Good," said Manny. "The keyboard will be our little secret. What do you say we meet at my house Friday after school?"

***

On Friday afternoon the three friends were sitting in Manny's kitchen. The keyboard lay between them on the table. "You know," said Manny, "this keyboard could really help us out with our school work."

"How do you figure?" asked Richie.

"Well," said Manny, "I've been having a little trouble with geometry."

"That's an understatement!" said Cheryl. She and Manny were in the same math class.

Manny ignored her. "Anyway, I was reading about this guy Euclid. He was an ancient Greek mathematician who wrote a book called *Elements of Geometry*."

"So you want to learn math from the

master, huh?" asked Richie.

"Well, why not?" replied Manny.

"No problem," said Richie, grabbing the keyboard. "How do you spell Euclid?"

"E-U-C-L-I-D," said Cheryl.

Seconds later, the great mathematician stood before them. He looked around, then began talking and gesturing with his hands.

"Whoa, what's he saying?" asked

Manny, startled.

Cheryl began to laugh. "What's the matter, Manny? Don't you understand ancient Greek?"

"Man, I didn't think of that," said Manny, grabbing the keyboard. He looked at Euclid. "Later, dude," he said as Euclid disappeared.

"Well," said Cheryl, "I guess we'll have to stick with time-travelers who speak English."

"I don't know," said Richie. "I was just thinking—it would be cool to bring back Sequoyah."

"Who?" asked Manny.

"He developed the Cherokees' written language," explained Cheryl. "Do you speak any Cherokee, Richie?"

"No, but Sequoyah could teach me," Richie replied. "Manny's right. This keyboard could help us learn all kinds of stuff."

"Come to think of it, there are people I'd like to bring back, too," said Cheryl.

"I have a paper due next week on the women's suffrage movement. Susan B. Anthony could help me write it. Or Elizabeth Cady Stanton." Noting Manny's puzzled expression, she added, "They helped women get the right to vote."

"Those people all sound pretty interesting," said Manny to his friends. "And we should bring them back—one of these days. But it's Friday afternoon. The weekend is here! It's time to have fun! Let's bring back someone who'll entertain us!"

"Hey, you just gave me a great idea," said Cheryl. "You guys are going to Tomoko's birthday party tonight, right?" The guys nodded. "Well, how's this for a birthday present? We bring the entertainment!"

"Cool!" said Richie. "But who should we bring?"

"What about some of those old-time rock 'n roll stars?" asked Manny. "Remember that documentary we watched on TV, Richie? With the Rolling Stones and all those weird bands from the 1960s?"

"That's a great idea, Manny!" said Cheryl. "We can put together a 1960s supergroup. Tomoko will flip out!"

"Let's do it!" said Manny.

***

Several hours later, Tomoko was

thanking the three friends for her birthday present.

"That was the best birthday gift I ever got. Thanks, you guys," she said.

"You're welcome," said Cheryl. "We're glad you liked it."

"And we're glad your basement is soundproofed!" added Manny. "The neighbors might not have enjoyed tonight's show."

"Where did you find those performers?" asked Tomoko. "The guy who played Jimi Hendrix was awesome. And those costumes! Is that what bell-bottoms really looked like?"

"Yeah, can you believe people really wore those things?" asked Richie.

"We'd better get going," said Cheryl, slinging her backpack with the keyboard inside over her shoulder. "See you on Monday, Tomoko."

Outside Manny turned to the others. "Just call us the party pros!" he said happily.

Chapter · 5

After school on Monday, Manny, Richie, and Cheryl were back in Cheryl's basement.

"Uh, listen you guys," said Richie. "There's something I'd better tell you."

"What's up?" Manny asked.

Richie cleared his throat nervously. He ran his fingers through his hair and looked away from his friends.

"I told Antoine Jackson about the keyboard," Richie mumbled.

"You what?!?" cried Cheryl.

"He was at Tomoko's birthday party," said Richie. "I didn't know this, but he's actually into 1960s music. He couldn't believe how much those 'actors' looked

and sounded like the real thing. He asked me what was up, and, well, I guess I told him."

"Oh man, I don't believe you!" cried Cheryl angrily.

"Chill out for a second, Cheryl," said Manny. "Do you think Antoine believed you, Richie?"

"No," said Richie. "In fact, he's been teasing me about it for days. He's really starting to get on my nerves."

"Then no harm done, right, Cheryl?"

asked Manny, turning towards the girl.

"I guess not," said Cheryl. "But Richie, you better tell Antoine you were only kidding. Hopefully that will be the end of it, okay?"

"Okay," agreed Richie.

"Now," said Manny. "Can we discuss the next party? That is what we're here to talk about, right?"

"Right," said Cheryl. "And Manny, it's your turn to go to the Party Committee meeting tomorrow. This time they want us to come up with our own idea for a party. I was thinking a sports theme might be fun."

"Great idea," said Richie. "We can bring back some old sports stars."

"Yeah!" said Manny. "Like Kareem Abdul Jabar and Joe Montana."

"And Martina Navratilova," Cheryl chimed in.

"And Billy Mills," said Richie. "He was a Lakota Sioux track star who won a gold medal in the 1964 Olympics. Hey, maybe we can set up some kind of Olympic competition at the party! Everyone can run a race or something."

"Sounds good," said Manny. "I think the committee will go for a sports party. So listen you guys, have you thought about what you're doing for the sophomore science fair? I can't think of anything good."

"Why not, Einstein?" teased Cheryl.

"Cheryl, that's it!" cried Manny.

"What's it?" asked Richie.

Manny smiled. "We'll bring back Albert Einstein! We can call him our 'living science exhibit.' We'll get him to talk about his theory of relativity."

"Think he'd go for it?" asked Richie.

"Let's find out," said Manny. He jumped up and went back toward Cheryl's uncle's lab. A minute later he returned with the keyboard. "Here goes," he said. Manny started typing.

When Einstein appeared, the wild-haired scientist stared at the kids for a minute with a dazed look. Then he noticed the keyboard. "Zack?" the puzzled scientist asked.

"Zack's my uncle," said Cheryl, surprised.

"You have his keyboard?" asked Einstein.

"Wait," said Richie. "You knew Cheryl's uncle, Dr. Einstein?"

"Yes," the great scientist replied. "When he developed the keyboard I was the first person he brought into the future."

"It makes sense," said Cheryl. "Your theory of relativity is all about time and

space, isn't it, Dr. Einstein?"

"Yes indeed," replied Einstein. "Tell me, what year is it now?"

"2075," said Manny.

"I met Zack in 2042. That's when he brought me here to the future. He's a brilliant man, your uncle," said Einstein to Cheryl. "Is he here?"

"I'm sorry," said Cheryl, "but my uncle died in 2043. That's why you never heard from him again."

"I see," said Einstein. He was quiet for a minute, and then asked, "Are the three of you carrying on with Zack's work?"

"Well, sort of," said Manny.

"You know, Dr. Einstein, we still have my uncle's books and a lot of his lab equipment," said Cheryl. "You're welcome to look at it if you want. In fact, why don't you stick around for a few days? You could sleep down here on the pull-out couch."

"I would be interested in seeing Zack's

laboratory. Thank you, Miss . . . ?"

"Oh, I'm Cheryl, and these are my friends Richie and Manny," Cheryl replied.

Einstein shook hands with everyone. "It's a pleasure to know you," he said.

"Oh, you'll get to know us a lot better in the next few days!" said Manny.

Chapter · 6

The next day after school, Manny and Einstein were discussing computer technology at Cheryl's kitchen table. Cheryl was sitting with them, but she wasn't paying attention.

"Where's Richie?" she asked, annoyed. "He was supposed to be here an hour ago to finish planning the sports party."

"We have to talk about the science fair, too," said Manny. "Dr. Einstein, we could really use your help."

"Of course," replied Einstein. "What can I do?"

Manny opened his mouth to answer, when two figures outside the kitchen window caught his eye.

"Uh-oh," he said. "Here comes trouble."

"Richie's here?" asked Cheryl.

"Yup," said Manny. "But he's not alone. Antoine's with him."

"Oh, no," cried Cheryl. "Dr. Einstein, I'm sorry, but you'd better stay down in the basement. And take the keyboard with you!"

"Cheryl, I've been thinking," said Manny. "What's the big deal if Antoine sees the keyboard? He's a cool guy. I don't think he'd tell anyone."

"You didn't think Richie would tell anyone, either," Cheryl replied.

"I say, if he wants to see the keyboard, we let him see it," said Manny.

"Fine," said Cheryl. "Why don't we just bring it to school and let everyone in on it?"

Before Manny could answer, the doorbell rang. Einstein headed down the basement stairs as Cheryl punched in the entrance code to release the bolt on the back door. The door swung open and in walked Richie and Antoine.

"Hey, Cheryl," said Antoine. "What's up, Manny?" Antoine noticed the keyboard, which was lying next to Manny's portable computer on the kitchen table. He turned to Richie. "Is that it?" he asked.

Richie looked guiltily at Cheryl.

58

"Oh, go ahead," said Cheryl. "I guess it's no big deal."

"So you guys are all in on this little game, huh?" asked Antoine, sitting at the table. "Can I play, too?"

"I told Antoine he could try the keyboard," said Richie. "He promised not to tell anyone."

"Go for it," said Manny. "Type in the name of the person you want to bring back from the past. Then hit ENTER. Why don't you bring back one of those twentieth century music acts you like so much? Type in that pelvis guy."

"You mean Elvis Presley?" asked Antoine. "Nah. I want to meet somebody tough and powerful, somebody like Genghis Khan."

"No way!" said Cheryl.

"Genghis who?" asked Manny.

"The founder of the Mongol Empire, man," said Antoine. "Back around the year 1200 Genghis was a fearsome warrior. He tried to conquer the world!"

Antoine typed madly.

"Stop typing, man," said Richie. "You're asking for. . ."

But it was too late! Antoine had hit ENTER. The gang heard the familiar hum and pop, and there stood the terrifying Mongolian warrior, holding a long sword in his hand.

Genghis wheeled around, confused and angry.

"Upstairs! Quick!" Cheryl cried. The gang ran through the living room and up the stairs to Cheryl's bedroom.

"Oh, man!" said Antoine, "I don't believe it. I swear I didn't think it would really work."

"Where's the keyboard?" Cheryl cried.

"I left it downstairs," said Antoine.

"You what?!?" yelled Manny.

The kids could hear Genghis yelling downstairs.

"We've got to get that keyboard and send Genghis back," said Richie.

"I'll do it," said Antoine. "After all it's

my fault he's here."

"We'll have to wait until Khan goes into another room or something. It sounds like he's running around down there," said Manny.

"Maybe he's trying to find a way out," said Richie.

"The doors are bolted," said Cheryl. "They only open with the code."

Suddenly, there was a loud crash,

then silence. After several minutes, the gang crept downstairs to investigate.

The big picture window in the living room was shattered.

"He escaped!" cried Cheryl.

Richie pointed to Genghis's sword lying on the carpet next to the couch. "Looks like he dropped something," Richie said.

"Quick," cried Manny. "Let's get the keyboard."

He ran into the kitchen, but was back seconds later with a terrible look on his face.

"The keyboard's gone!" Manny cried.

Chapter · 7

"Oh, no," said Richie. "Now what do we do?"

"Quick!" cried Cheryl, punching in the release code for the front door. "Let's see if we can find Genghis!"

The kids rushed outside. A few seconds later, Dr. Einstein dashed out behind them. In her haste, Cheryl had left the door open. "What's happening?" asked the startled scientist. "I heard a commotion. Is everything all right?"

Manny explained that Antoine had brought back Genghis Khan by mistake. "Now Genghis is gone," Manny continued, "and so is the keyboard! We've go to figure out what to . . ."

"Look!" cried Antoine, pointing to the street.

An open-air solarbus was passing by. In the back stood Genghis, its only passenger.

"Ghenghis Khan must have seen the

bus at the corner and jumped on board," said Richie.

"He's headed into town!" cried Cheryl.

"Won't the driver notice his passenger is rather unusual?" asked Einstein.

"Solarbuses don't have drivers," explained Cheryl. "They're run by computers."

"We've got to get downtown!" said Antoine. "When's the next bus?"

"Not for another ten minutes," answered Cheryl. "We'll have to wait."

The gang headed to the corner bus stop. Antoine apologized the whole way.

"I should have believed you, Richie," he said. "You've always been straight with me."

"Forget it, Antoine," said Richie. "What's done is done."

"Besides," added Manny, "it is pretty unbelievable—a keyboard that brings people back from the past."

"You know," said Cheryl, "we probably shouldn't have messed with the keyboard in the first place. Something like this was bound to happen."

The gang waited in silence for a few minutes. Then Manny said, "What I can't figure out is why Genghis took the keyboard."

"Maybe he thought it was a weapon," said Richie.

"Antoine was holding it when Genghis appeared," said Cheryl. "Genghis

probably thought it had some kind of importance."

"Here comes the bus," said Einstein. Moments later, the gang was on their way into town.

***

Rockville's town center was in an uproar. Store windows were broken, and a newsstand and a fruit and vegetable stand had been completely destroyed. People were running around

in all directions. Things were a mess.

Richie spied a police officer and asked her what was going on.

"We're not sure," the police officer replied. "There's some kind of maniac on the loose. One woman said he looked like he was from another world."

"She got that right," mumbled Manny.

"How did all this stuff get trashed?" asked Richie.

"There was a big stampede here a few minutes ago," replied the police officer. "Apparently, this crazy guy just got off the bus and started yelling and chasing people. He grabbed a man's cane and was swinging it around like a sword!"

"Was anyone hurt?" asked Antoine nervously.

"Luckily not," said the officer. "Now why don't you kids clear out of here? We have work to do."

The group started to walk away, when Manny moaned, "Oh no!" He pointed to the Organic Produce sign that lay

trampled on the ground. The keyboard was crushed beneath it!

Five minutes later, the gang was sitting under a tree in front of the post office. Einstein was turning the keyboard around in his hands, assessing the damage.

"Well, I guess that settles it," said Manny. "We've got to get rid of Genghis."

"But how?" asked Richie.

"If I bring the keyboard back to Zack's lab, I may be able to fix it," said Einstein. "I only hope I can do it before something really terrible happens."

Chapter · 8

Manny agreed to return to Cheryl's house and help Einstein while the others remained in town.

"Where and when should we meet?" asked Manny.

"Let's meet right here," replied Richie. "Does an hour give you enough time, Dr. Einstein?"

"It will have to," Einstein replied. "I don't think we can risk more time than that. Even if time is relative."

Manny and Einstein left on the solarbus. Cheryl, Antoine and Richie started wandering around. When they got back to the town center, the three stopped and stared.

There were newscasters, cameras, and lights everywhere. Rockville was in a state of confusion. A reporter noticed the kids standing in a huddle. "You kids better beat it," he said. "Don't you know there's a maniac on the loose?"

Just then a voice could be heard over a loudspeaker. "He's headed into the park!" the voice announced.

"You two go ahead," said Richie. "I'll stay here and wait for Manny and Dr. Einstein. Be cool, you guys."

"You too, man," said Antoine.

Cheryl and Antoine headed for the

park, which was two blocks away. The whole park area was surrounded by armed police.

"What if they shoot Genghis Khan?" asked Cheryl.

"We've just got to keep our fingers crossed," said Antoine.

"But what happens to history if Genghis Khan disappears in Rockville Center?" Cheryl cried. "What about the Mongol Empire? Who's going to sweep across the world in the twelfth century? I mean what about all the history books? Are we going to end up in them? I can see it now: Cheryl Pinter, Manny Trujillo, Richie Adair and Antoine Jackson— history hackers!"

Antoine groaned. "All right, all right. Let's try to see if we can track Genghis ourselves."

"If we can just keep tabs on him until Manny and Dr. Einstein get back," Cheryl said, "maybe we won't change the course of history."

A police officer neared and the pair ducked behind some camera equipment. Cheryl and Antoine could hear the police talking over their radios. It seemed that Genghis had holed up inside the park.

Cheryl looked at Antoine and pointed towards the park. Antoine nodded. They slowly crept along, hiding behind the camera equipment until they reached a line of bushes.

Cheryl lead the way as they crawled behind the bushes and into the park.

Without warning, she stopped. Antoine bumped right into her. "Look!" she hissed.

Straight ahead was a huge rock. The Mongol warrior was crouched behind it, with his back to the two teens.

Suddenly there was a loud cackling sound. "Attention!" a voice from behind Cheryl and Antoine boomed, "come out with your hands up!"

"Listen!" said Antoine, "it's the police on the loudspeaker."

"Look out!" cried Cheryl.

Genghis Khan had wheeled around in the direction of the booming announcement. That's when he saw the teens.

The fearsome warrior growled and pulled out a sharp dagger from his belt. He roared and leaped towards Cheryl and Antoine.

"Run!" Cheryl screamed.

"Where?" Antoine screamed back. They were boxed in by the line of bushes.

Suddenly, a voice made Cheryl jump. "We're baaack!" whispered Manny, popping up from behind the bushes. Richie and Dr. Einstein crowded in behind him.

"What's up with the keyboard?" yelled Cheryl, frantically.

"They don't call Albert Einstein a genius for nothing," Manny replied. Einstein handed the keyboard over to Manny.

"There's no time for a science chat," said Antoine. The Mongol warrior was closing in. "Give me that thing!" he cried. Manny tossed him the keyboard.

Antoine quickly typed in the

GENGHIS KHAN and hit DELETE.

"Please, please work," he whispered.

"Check it out!" Cheryl cheered. Confused voices came over the loudspeaker.

"Where'd that guy go?"

"He was just there—I saw him!"

"It's like he vanished into thin air!"

The kids slapped each other on the back. "We did it!" said Manny.

"Let's get out of here," said Richie.

The group headed away from the park and all the commotion. They walked in silence until they came to a quiet street. After a while Manny spoke.

"Wasn't that incredible?" he asked.

"You said it," agreed Cheryl. "Dr. Einstein, thank you for fixing the keyboard."

"I'm glad I was able to help," Einstein replied. "And now, all of you can help me. I'd like to go back to my own time."

"Sure thing Dr. Einstein," said Manny. "Are you ready?"

"Yes," replied Einstein. "Thank you for a very exciting trip to the future. But from now on, I think I'll be content to stay in my own time. Please be careful with the keyboard—if you choose to use it again. Goodbye."

"Goodbye, Dr. Einstein," said Cheryl, typing on the keyboard. "Thank you for

everything." With that, Cheryl hit the DELETE key and Einstein was gone.

"What do you think he meant, 'if we choose to use the keyboard again'?" asked Manny.

"Face it, man," said Richie. "That keyboard is trouble. I vote from now on we let the past stay in the past."

"I'm with you," said Cheryl. "Manny, what do you say?"

"Well . . . ," said Manny. "What do you think, Antoine?"

"Are you kidding?" replied Antoine. "I've learned my lesson!"

The teens all looked at each other. Then Cheryl threw the keyboard on the ground and jumped on top of it. Manny and Antoine took turns doing the same. Richie grabbed the keyboard and began pulling out all its wires. "Just to be on the safe side," he said.

"Well, one thing's for sure," Manny sighed. "That keyboard is 'history!' "